Zain Bhikha

Allah Made Everything
The Song Book

Illustrated by Azra Momin

THE ISLAMIC FOUNDATION

Allah Made Everything: The Song Book

First Published in 2018 by
The Islamic Foundation
2nd impression, 2018

Distributed by
Kube Publishing Ltd
MCC, Ratby Lane, Markfield
Leicestershire, LE67 9SY
United Kingdom
Tel: +44 (0) 1530 249230, Fax +44 (0) 1530 249656
E-Mail: info@kubepublishing.com
Website: **www.kubepublishing.com**

Text and Lyrics © Zain Bhikha
Illustrations © Azra Momin

In partnership with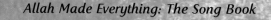

www.zeebeekids.com & ™ Zain Bhikha Studios

Zeebee Kids, A division of Zain Bhikha Studios

Author: Zain Bhikha
Illustrator: Azra Momin

A Catalogue-in-Publication Data record is available from the British Library

ISBN 978-0-86037-770-2

Printed in Istanbul, Turkey by Mega Basim

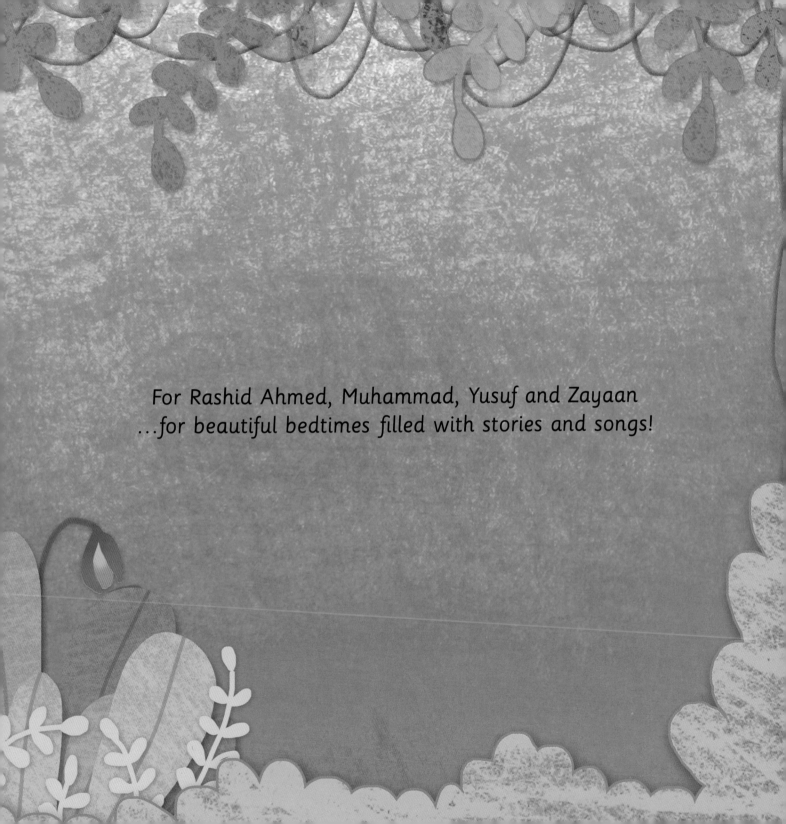

For Rashid Ahmed, Muhammad, Yusuf and Zayaan
…for beautiful bedtimes filled with stories and songs!

Hey little fish at the bottom of the ocean

Moving along in a really cool motion

Did you ever wonder where you came from

Who is the Lord

of all Creation?

The little fish said
" That's my Lord!
Allah the Creator of us all "

Hey little bird so way up high
Light up the sky
with your colour design

Tell me who made you and I
Me to walk and you to fly?

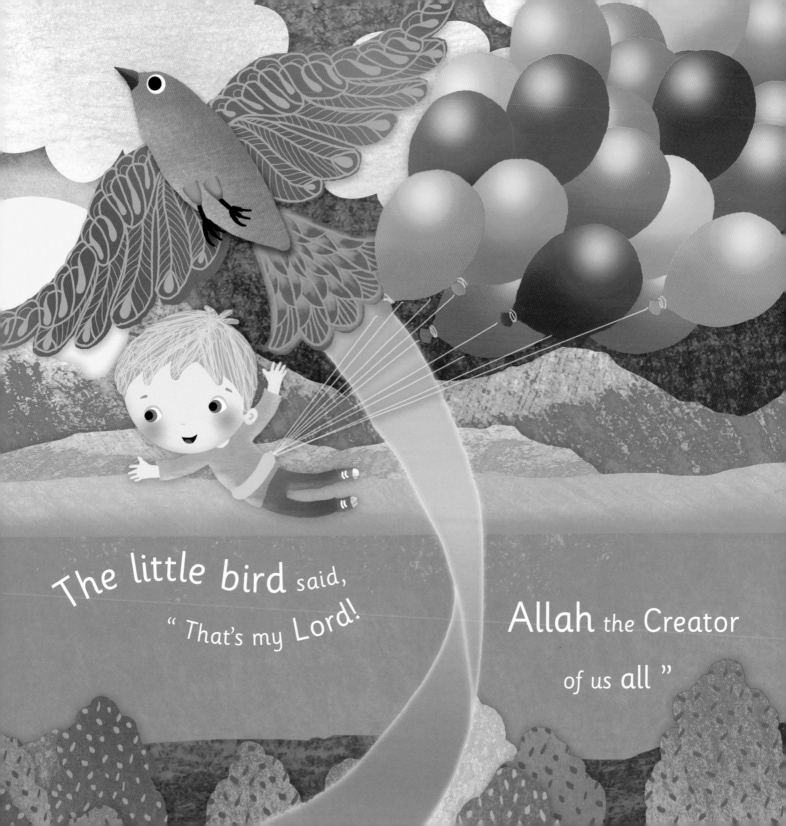

The little bird said, "That's my Lord!

Allah the Creator of us all"

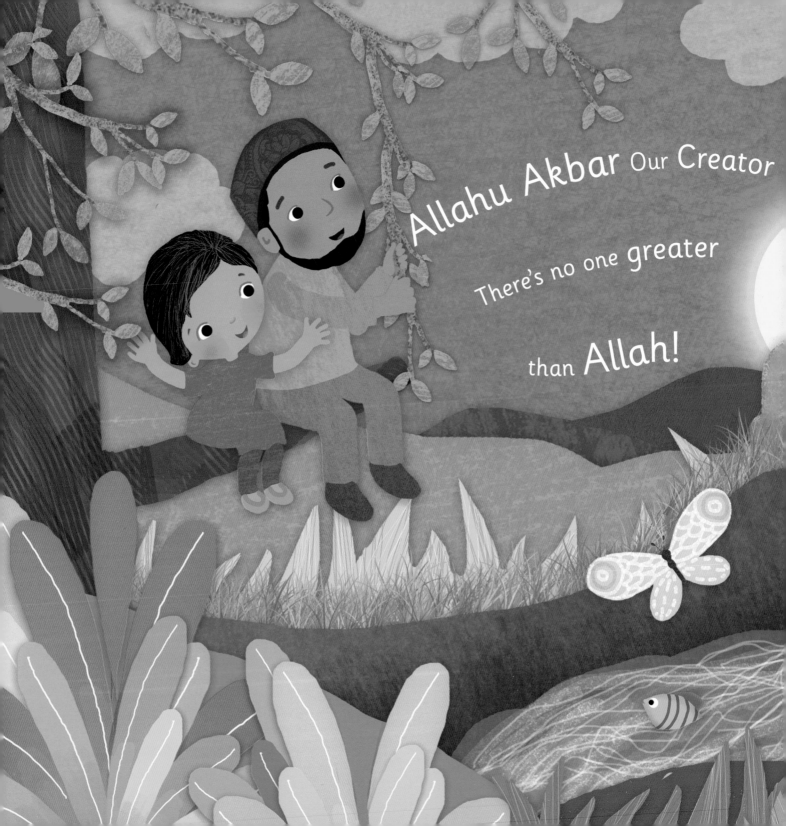

Allahu Akbar Our Creator

There's no one greater

than Allah!

So why do we stand tall
Too proud to recognise
What's right before our eyes
Signs from our Lord

Hey alligator laying so still
Who's your Maker, by who's will
Do you crawl and do you swim
Who controls everything?

But who is the one that you rely on
Life or death, who is deciding?
The lion said
" That's my Lord!
Allah the Creator of us all "

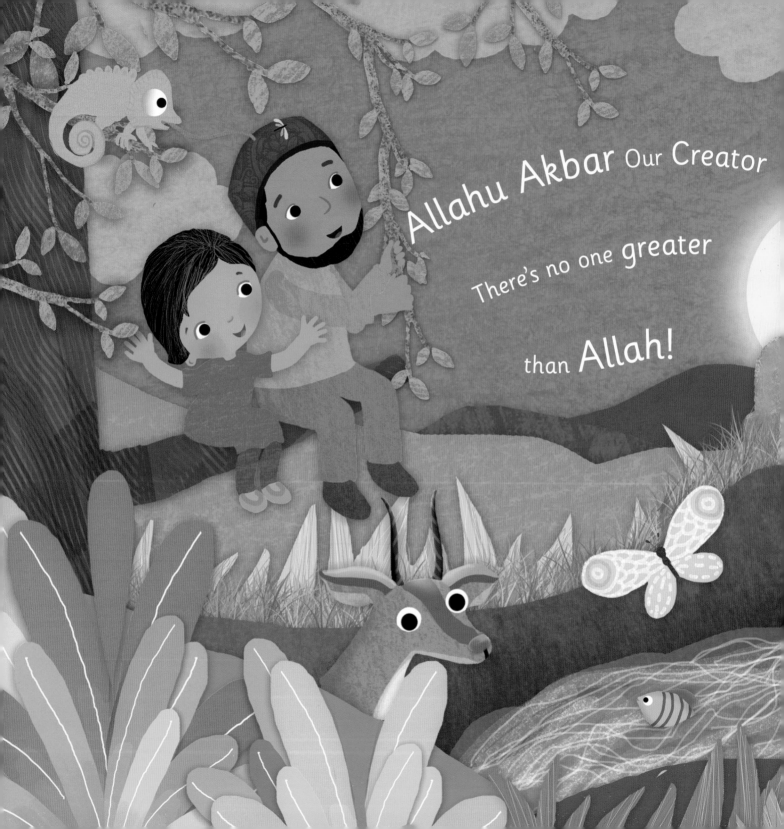

Allahu Akbar Our Creator

There's no one greater

than Allah!

So why do we stand tall
Too proud to recognise
What's right before our eyes
Signs from our Lord

Hey my brother
Hey my sister

See yourself as self-sustainer
But don't you see
what will come later

We all return
to the Creator!

TOP SOIL

WHO REALLY MAKES PLANTS GROW

FACTS

Then we'll say

" That's my Lord!

Oh Allah,
Forgive us all "

I travelled the world
north to the south

East to the west
and there is no doubt

Whoever I see
whatever I've found

I can hear them
sing out loud

Alhamdullillāh
Praise my Lord!

Allah the Creator of us all

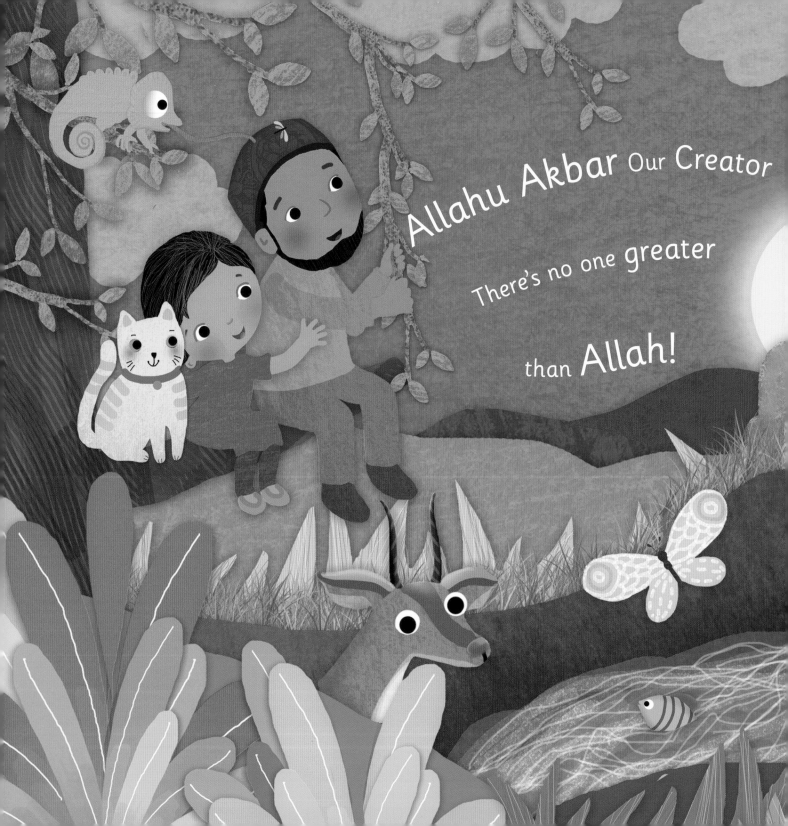

Allahu Akbar Our Creator

There's no one greater

than Allah!

So why do we stand tall
Too proud to recognise
What's right before our eyes
Signs from our Lord

Allah made everything
You and I

Allah made everything
The earth and the blue sky

Do we **remember** Him

Thank Him for everything

Surrender to only Him

With all **our lives**

About Zain Bhikha

Zain Bhikha has served as an inspiration to people the world over since he first began his singing in 1994. He is well-loved by fans young and old and remains amongst the most popular Islamic artists.

With more than a dozen albums to his name, Zain's songs have graced homes throughout the world and touched people's lives in uplifting and often profound ways. He has been described as an influential global peace and unity ambassador.

Zain's loyal fans have followed his career over more than two decades and his audience continues to grow in his country of birth, South Africa as well as globally. His albums have been launched in all major cities and he has performed across most continents.

The song-book, "Allah made Everything" is the first in a series of printed and illustrated books under Zain Bhikha's: "ZeeBee Kids" label. Zain's passion for teaching and uplifting the lives of young children towards God-consciousness has been at the centre of many of his albums, plays and youth workshops. The natural evolution to print, live shows, Apps and other media forums under the exciting ZeeBee kids umbrella is yet another way that Zain remains a pioneer in his field.

Zain Bhikha resides in Johannesburg, South Africa where he enjoys spending quality time with his wife and four sons.

About Azra Momin

Azra Momin paints, makes textile art and jewelry, illustrates books, and writes for magazines, not necessarily in that order. She enjoys playing made-up games and going geocaching with her favorite comrades - her husband and daughter. A stack of children's books and mystery novels is always by her side, and she dreams about living in an earth ship. Find her work on Instagram @azramomin.